Simon Lacks Self-discipline

G! Bongo! Bongo! Edition

Mae Chelle M. Medina

Ukiyoto Publishing

All global publishing rights are held by

Ukiyoto Publishing

Published in 2024

Content Copyright © Mae Chelle M. Medina

ISBN 9789362697387

All rights reserved.

No part of this publication may be reproduced, transmitted, or stored in a retrieval system, in any form by any means, electronic, mechanical, photocopying, recording or otherwise, without the prior permission of the publisher.

The moral rights of the author have been asserted.

This is a work of fiction. Names, characters, businesses, places, events, locales, and incidents are either the products of the author's imagination or used in a fictitious manner. Any resemblance to actual persons, living or dead, or actual events is purely coincidental.

This book is sold subject to the condition that it shall not by way of trade or otherwise, be lent, resold, hired out or otherwise circulated, without the publisher's prior consent, in any form of binding or cover other than that in which it is published.

www.ukiyoto.com

Dedication

This storybook is dedicated to all my previous and future students, *Basti, Catherine, Cassidy, Lily, Ally, Sebby, Coral, JJ, Alex, Christian, Andres, William, Wilson, Gabriel, Leon and Titus*

To my parents, *Celso and Emelita*

To *Jett and Michelle*

To my sister from another mother, *Nicky*

To my very kind and patient illustrator, *Jay Ambanta (jayambanta@gmail.com)*

To the bookstores where I purchase my pre-loved copies, *Kyle A. and Mhelyn*

To Ukiyoto Publishing and Team, *Maraming salamat!*
Thank you for all the courage and inspiration.

Synopsis:

G! Bongo! Bongo! is the hottest mobile game in town because it can earn you a Super Genius reputation once you collect the highest number of shooting stars.

Red Hot Caution: "Free access to the game requires a minimum playtime of three hours daily; otherwise, your arrow will be placed in the freezing zone where it can never be moved or touched."

Simon is turning Grade 1 this year. It is the beginning of the new school year, and as early as the second day of class, he is already punished by Mr. Gates.

Can Simon maintain his Super Genius reputation while surviving the school year without failing grades?"

Contents

Chapter 1 *G!Bongo! Bongo!*	1
Chapter 2 "Welcome Simon, The Persimmon"	3
Chapter 3 Simon is sanctioned by Mr. Gates	11
Chapter 4 Simon's Math Quiz Received a Huge Skeleton Red Egg	13
About the Author	17

Chapter 1
G! Bongo! Bongo!
Red Hot Caution

Simon Lacks Self-discipline

Hello friends, my name is Simon. I am 6 years old and ranked 21st on the worldwide charts of the G! BONGO! BONGO! Super G! Players Honor Roll.

"G! BONGO! BONGO!" is the hottest mobile game because I can take hold of this bony arrow and take aim at any **BONGO! BONGO!**, *the technical name* of the shooting star located on Planet G!

Each star is owned by a powerful sorceress who can grant me 3 wishes, such as giving me free stars to upgrade my arrow. And, I really want that fiery red arrow with a shade of blue.

However, it gets tricky sometimes because of this **"Red Hot Caution"** that flashes once in a while: **"WARNING! In order to continue using your arrow, each player must play for a minimum of 3 hours daily; otherwise, we will place your arrow in the freezing zone where it can never be moved or touched."**

Chapter 2
"Welcome Simon, The Persimmon"

*B**ut tonight is not Simon's regular Sunday; tomorrow is Monday,* **his first day of school**. *It's the* beginning of the new school year.

Simon is already preparing to sleep, lying in his bed, running his little fingers over the softness of his 110% pure cotton quilt, which his mom bought directly from the factory.

You might be curious about the 110% pure cotton quilt. Well, there's a bit of science to it.

Simon's mom grew up believing that having a good night's sleep before the first day of school is a good omen. It means that if Simon wakes up bright and chirpy on the first day of school, it will bring him a school year of good fortune. No failing grades, no nearly failing grades, but almost perfect scores in all subjects.

Believe it or not, Simon shares the same belief. So, he turns off the light, shuts his eyes, and starts counting shooting stars from 1 to 100.

Until there is a sudden sound coming from his phone, where the tune goes, ***"G! BONGO! BONGO!", "G! BONGO! BONGO!", "G! BONGO! BONGO!"***

Simon Lacks Self-discipline

Simon shuts his eyes tightly, trying his best to ignore the reminder to play, yet the sound grows louder and louder.

Suddenly, he jumps out of bed, reaches for his phone, and remembers that today **he hasn't played for 3 full hours**. The horror of having his trustworthy arrow frozen gives him such a fright that **he cannot simply ignore it**.

Additionally, **the thought of descending from the 21st rank on the Super G! Players Honor Roll is already hurting his ego**.

He started swiping and pressing buttons on his phone. After finding the *G! BONGO! BONGO! game application*, he immediately entered his **gamer details**:

BONGO USER NAME: PERSIMMON
PASSWORD: NOMMISREP

WELCOME SIMON, THE PERSIMMON

The welcoming note lifted his worries, and he felt much relieved. He said to himself, *"I promise, I will only play for 2 hours, no more jolly good 5-minute extensions. Let me set an alarm."*

"Zzzzzz! Quack! Quaaaaaaaccckkkkk!" The alarm clock started ringing. He had been playing for 2 hours, yet Simon swiped up and chose ***SNOOZE***. *(History repeated itself until he felt the numbing of his thumbs,* ***and that's when he realized it was already 2 AM!)***

zzz! quack! quaaaacccckkk!

In panic, he stopped playing and immediately lay down to sleep.

Simon opens his left eye and tries to make sense of the time. "The short hand is pointing towards 6 and the long hand is on 10," he thinks. ***"What time is*** *it?"* In shock, he says the time out loud, **"It is now 6:50 AM." "Goodness gracious, my class starts at 7 AM!"**

Furious, he descends downstairs, calling for his mom. **"Mooooom! Mom, where are you? You didn't wake me up? Where is my school uniform?" I won't bathe anymore; I'll just change into my school uniform."** (*His lips form a circular motion, pointing to his school uniform.*)

Mom remains silent, without a word or disapproving expression, as she hands him his school uniform. Simon, in contrast, reacts like a bolt of lightning, immediately changing into it upon reaching for it.

He failed to comb his hair.

He failed to brush his teeth.

He failed to wear his socks.

Simon's hands are colder than the North Pole, and his palms are starting to sweat. He harshly opens the door of their house, causing a loud *"Baaaaang"* as it hits the wall, and starts running in the direction of his school. Luckily, his school is only 15 minutes away from his house.

Without a doubt, Simon is 10 minutes late for class. It is now 7:10 AM, and today is his first day of school.

He enters his designated classroom, drenched in his own sweat. His school uniform seems freshly laundered, but the fabric conditioner smells like old clothes that have been worn five times that week and haven't been washed; it's awful.

Everyone starts talking behind him; some secretly share laughs due to his foul odour, while others judge his hair, likening it to an angry cactus. One even speaks to him, saying, *"Socks aren't really expensive, you know? Why don't you ask your mommy to buy you some pairs?"*

But you know what? Simon ignored his first lesson of the school year.

In fact, in his mind, he thinks that everyone is behind him, **_condescendingly_**. *"Fine, fine, all your noses can judge my smell all you want, but none of you are on the same level as mine. I am ranked 21ST in the Super G! Players Honor Roll.* I have a tremendous amount of shooting stars. *I am a* *genius! Almost a genius, fra-la-la-la la-la! la-la! la-la!"*

"The singing of *'fra-la-la-la la-la! la-la! la-la!'* merrily continued until he reached home at around 3 PM. Despite his outward jolliness, deep inside, he knew that he had betrayed his mom's trust by not being a disciplined child that day. In silence and guilt, he opened their door, preparing for his mom's lecture.

The kitchen door suddenly creaked open, and a voice was heard saying, **"Son, don't forget to complete your school assignment. I read from the bulletin** *(Grade 1 parents' chat group)* **that you have a Math quiz and assignment due tomorrow. Call me if you need help."**

"Aha! Mom is not angry! he he he!" Simon uttered in a low voice. Unfortunately, his mom's reminder faded into the air, joining the swirling dust to nothingness. His mom's sincerity in not scolding Simon for what transpired that morning, hoping he would realize his mistakes, went utterly unappreciated.

Simon rushed to his room, hoping to nap because he was tremendously sleepy. As soon as he lay down, he fell asleep. It wasn't until 9 PM that he finally woke up and sat at his study table."

Sitting down, he is torn between two options:

[A] To answer and study his math assignment; or,

[B] To join the *"magical night"* at *G! Bongo! Bongo!* as they witness the *BONGO! SHOOO SHOOO TRAIN* transporting the newest magical tools. *"I heard that tonight will be the launch of the wildest arrows ever, a magical upgrade of a lifetime."*

The option was a no-brainer; we all knew that Simon would choose to be present at tonight's magical "shoo shoo" train online party.

On the other hand, Simon promised himself, *"I'll just spend 3 hours; isn't 3 hours just a small fraction of the night? It won't hurt. And then, I promise, I will do my math homework."* Midnight has passed, but no matter how loud the *"Zzzzzz! quack! quaaaaaaccckkkk!"* gets, it is hardly ignored. History repeats itself; he feels his thumbs numbing, and it is now 2 AM. He fell asleep without completing his designated homework.

zzz! quack! quaaaaccccckkk!

Chapter 3
Simon is sanctioned by Mr. Gates

"*Today is Tuesday. Simon wakes up at exactly 7:05AM. He immediately changed into his school uniform, no socks.*"

As soon as he enters the gate, a school staff member asks for his name. *"What is your name? Please hand me your School I.D.,"* the staff member demands. Simon is scared, feeling like a mouse caught by a German shepherd; his hairs is starting to get prickly due to shame and fright.

Upon surrendering his school I.D., the school staff member introduces himself. *"I am Mr. Gates, the school's disciplinarian. It is my obligation to discipline tardy students. Mr. Simon Persimmon, you are late to school for two consecutive days now."*

Continuing, Mr. Gates says, *"In this school, we do not tolerate tardiness; in fact, we condemn and sanction it. As you choose not to be self-disciplined, your penalty is to:*

"STAND UNDER THE SUN FOR 15 MINUTES."

"If you feel the punishment is extreme or unjustified, you may lodge your concern in writing, addressing it to Mrs. Guidy, our school's Guidance Counselor."

Simon is profusely sweating while standing under the sun. He cannot discern the source of his anxiety: Is it because of the shame of being punished, or knowing that dried sweat will make him stink again, or is it because, "based on my mental calculations, by the time I join Math class, it will be 7:20 AM? Surely, Mrs. Diviccione will give me some good scolding."

Chapter 4
Simon's Math Quiz Received a Huge Skeleton Red Egg

By the time he enters Mrs. Diviccione's class, she is already instructing everybody to *"pass your answer sheets, time's up, submit your papers."* There was a surprise quiz on multiplication and division. And, because Simon fails to take the quiz, she draws a huge skeleton red egg in front of his answer sheet.

After seeing the huge skeleton egg in color red, ***he wants to cry***, only that he is suppressing it. He has never felt so wrong and ashamed in his entire life. He is genuinely anxious about how to explain all these ruckuses to his mom, mainly because he knows that she will be saddened.

It takes him 40 minutes to arrive home from school. As soon as he enters the house, he searches for his mom. He finds her in the kitchen cooking the sweetest spaghetti sauce with a bunch of hotdogs, all for his snack.

And he starts to confess…

"Mom, this morning, I met our school's disciplinary officer, Mr. Gates, and I was penalized for being late to school. I stood under the sun for 15 minutes, which is why I missed my Math quiz and received a red skeleton egg from Mrs. Diviccione. **I failed my very first Math quiz.**"

"These past few days, **I've been busy spending 3-4 hours collecting arrows and shooting stars.** I easily give in to those little teasing notification sounds. I am not comfortable labeling it as an addiction, but I am addicted to playing that game. **Mom, what should I do then?**"

Mom looked at Simon; **a simple smile was her response.**

"Mom, please say something; you've only given me a smile. You are scaring me away. Please don't be too mad."

"Son, look, punishing you is not the solution to cure your 'sickness.' Even if I become strict and formulate various forms of punishments, do you honestly think that solves your concern? No. It will only make you dislike me."

"In fact, you know the answer more than me; I never play that game. Start with what caused your addiction. Playing mobile games is part of growing up; it's your generation's culture. So, the power of self-control and self-discipline rests in your hands and mind. If I trust you, my son, all the more you should trust yourself that you can resist temptations."

Upon hearing those words, Simon reaches for his mom's cheek and gives her a peck and says, **"Mommy, thank you!"**

During that night, he reaches for his phone; he did what he had to do, *uninstalling G! BONGO! BONGO! and said to himself, "there is time to play, time to study. I should be responsible for my actions because Mom trusts me. Growing up is challenging but exciting."*

16   Simon Lacks Self-discipline

<u>Reflection time</u>:

1. How many gaming hours in a day is considered reasonable?

2. Is neglecting to study in exchange for numerous gaming hours a good habit?

3. What moral lesson/s did you gain after reading and knowing Simon's struggle?

About the Author

Mae Chelle M. Medina

Mae Chelle M. Medina is a bilingual (English to Mandarin and vice versa) children's storybook and worksheet writer. One of her copyrighted works is titled 'Please Don't Bully Me! 《请别欺负我！》'.

She is a Hanyu Shuiping Kaoshi (汉语水平考试) HSK - Level 5 passer and a Certified HR Associate (CHRA) by HREAP. Besides writing storybooks for kids, she teaches and enjoys reading.

www.ingramcontent.com/pod-product-compliance
Lightning Source LLC
LaVergne TN
LVHW041644070526
838199LV00053B/3553